TULSA CITY-COUNTY LIBRARY

CAT VS. VAC

Written and Illustrated by
Kaz Windness

Ready-to-Read

Simon Spotlight

New York   London   Toronto   Sydney   New Delhi

SIMON SPOTLIGHT
An imprint of Simon & Schuster Children's Publishing Division
1230 Avenue of the Americas, New York, New York 10020
This Simon Spotlight edition August 2023
Text and illustrations copyright © 2023 by Kaz Windness
SIMON SPOTLIGHT, READY-TO-READ, and colophon are registered trademarks of
Simon & Schuster, Inc.
For information about special discounts for bulk purchases, please contact Simon &
Schuster Special Sales at 1-866-506-1949 or business@simonandschuster.com. The
Simon & Schuster Speakers Bureau can bring authors to your live event. For more
information or to book an event contact the Simon & Schuster Speakers Bureau at
1-866-248-3049 or visit our website at www.simonspeakers.com.
Manufactured in the United States of America 0723 LAK
10 9 8 7 6 5 4 3 2 1
This book has been catalogued by the Library of Congress
ISBN 978-1-6659-3718-4 (hc)
ISBN 978-1-6659-3717-7 (pbk)
ISBN 978-1-6659-3719-1 (ebook)

Door crack. Sunbeam.

Cat stretch. Daydream.

Big box. Small beak.

Pets push. Pets peek.

Dog run.

Cat hide.

Bad Bird.   Vac ride.

Vac VROOM,
Vac SCHLOOP!
Vac eat cat poop.

Vac chase. Dog WEE!

Vac GLURP dog pee.

Vac catch. Vac BITE.

Dog wail. Cat . . . FIGHT!

Cat tap. Vac grin.

Cord ZAP! Vac win.

Cat hiss. Hose out.

Vac traps dog snout.

Sad Bird frees friend.

Hose SLURP! Vac win.

Cat plan. Cat scheme.

Cat forms Pet Team!

Gray Rat. Green Snake.
Cage CLICK! Jailbreak!

Pets stalk.

Snake stretch.

Hey, Vac!

Vac trip. Bird free!

(So is dog pee.)

Door SLAM! Vac fly!

Eat grass, Vac Guy!

KNOCK-KNOCK!

It's back!

Pets join!
ATTACK!

BOOF! BAM!

KICK! PAW!

SWISH! SWOOSH!

HISS! CLAW!

Victory a click away . . .

Cat and Bird have saved the day!

DOG, CAT, BIRD, SNAKE,
SQUEAK-SQUAWK,
SHIMMY-SHAKE!

Sunbeam. Door crack.
Vac gone. Peace back.